Family Day

Written by
Emma Diaz Bradley
and Terry Diaz-Bradley

Illustrations by
Ana K. Quintero Villafraz

For my big sister and role model, Jane,
who has shown me what unconditional love means.
For Gram-gram, who always inspired me with her whimsical poems,
and for my Abuela, whose presence I have felt
from the Heavens my whole life.
Thank you all! ~ Emma

For my magical daughters, Jane and Emma,
who show me every day what it means
to be openminded and tenderhearted.
You are my everything! ~ TDB

ISBN: 978-1-7377412-0-6 (paperback)
ISBN: 978-1-7377412-1-3 (hardcover)
ISBN: 978-1-7377412-2-0 (ebook)

Family Day

Written by
Emma Diaz Bradley
and Terry Diaz-Bradley

Illustrations by
Ana K. Quintero Villafraz

In the happy village of Broodtown,
where summer comes straight off of spring,

the people who call this their hometown,
gather for Broodtown's Spring Fling.

They come, one and all, to the Town Square,
where there's food and arcade games galore,
and nobody would want to be elsewhere
for the festival the families adore.

Each family arrives with their loved ones.
Some walk and some ride their bikes.
Moms, dads, aunties, and grandmoms,
no two are exactly alike.

Their mayor is Mr. McPenny.
In Broodtown, he's very well known.
This village is home to so many,
each one from a family their own.

There's Ryan, raised by two mommies,
who was adopted right after his birth.
They already had brother Tommy,
the greatest big brother on Earth!

Now Jessica has just one Daddy,
and a grandmom who lives with her, too,
along with her twin sister, Maddie,
and a guinea pig named Kangaroo.

Oh, look! Now, there's little Leo,
whose parents are still in high school.
Together this close little trio
look happy and loving and cool.

Here we see Linda and Kenny,
their family is made up of two.
They work and they travel a-plenty,
and they even go to the zoo!

Behind them is sweet Mrs. Proctor,
who's raising her grandaughter, Sue,
while Mom and Dad work to help doctors
heal sick kids who live in Peru.

Who could ever miss sweet tiny Tessie!
She lives both at Mom's house and Dad's.
At Mom's is a poodle named Bessie.
At Dad's is a kitten named Tabs.

Now here comes the large Allen family,
all led by stepmom and stepdad.
They have six kids with big personalities,
who rarely, if ever, get mad.

Watch Ryan and Tommy race go-karts,
While Jessica hugs Kangaroo.

Little Leo drags Mom to do sand art,
as Linda and Kenny kazoo.

Mrs. Proctor buys Sue cotton candy,
while Tessie wins big at Ring Toss.

Being many comes in really handy,
When the Allens play a game of lacrosse.

As each family competes for the prizes,
As sure as the heavens above,

Big and small, and in all shapes and sizes,
Broodtown's families are bound by their love!

THE END

CPSIA information can be obtained
at www.ICGtesting.com
Printed in the USA
BVHW021115070222
628293BV00017B/549